FOR DARLA
& ANNALENA

Edited by
Amy Osmond
Cook

Photography: Johnny Beutler
Graphic Design: Paul Meshreky
Thanks to: Ben Bergeson, Tad Baltzer,
Rachel Struhs, Rebecca Richards,
Tyler Jacobs, Mark Howe,
Jill Walker, Colt & Abi Bowden,
Jennifer Sanders Peterson

Produced
by
Jon Berrett

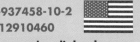

MUMBO JUMBO

ISBN 978-1-937458-10-2
LCCN 2012910460
Visit www.sourcedmediabooks.com.
Printed in the United States of America.

To the Schultz Family!

THE GOON HOLLER GUIDEBOOK

Written & Illustrated by Parker Jacobs
Created by Parker & Christian Jacobs

♡ Parker Jacobs

My name is Toobaloth C. Grassfoot. I am not a human. I am not a bear. I am not even a goon. I guess I'm what some folks call a yeti, a sasquatch, or a "Bigfoot." For many years, I have roamed the wilderness eating bark and discovering many strange and wonderful things that most people never get to see. I have walked and walked through the countryside, all the while being pestered by birds trying to build nests on my head, squirrels trying to hitch free rides on my fur, and people trying to stick me in a museum. One day, I tried to find a cave to take a nap in. I climbed a tree and got spooked by a hissing possum. So, I leaped from the tree and splashed through a waterfall, which was a secret portal that brought me to a new home called "Goon Holler." Goon Holler is full of magical creatures, music, adventure, and the best ice cream this side of Bergertucky. I want to share the fun with all my friends, so I've created this book about Goon Holler for you to explore until you can come and visit me in person. Enjoy!

THE GOON HOLLER AREA

- ○ **GOON HOLLER**
  Find out who's who, grab a snack, and explore the mines!

- ● **MAGIC TOWER**
  Learn the history of the Holler and the 3 lessons of magic!

- ● **THE STATION**
  Meet Dosie and learn to play Shoot'R Loser and the ukulele!

- ○ **CAHOOLSVILLE**
  Pick your favorite ice cream, visit the club, and learn a new joke!

- ○ **LUSHY LAKE**
  Take a vacation! Ride the rides! Learn about underwater creatures!

- ○ **TURKEY PEAK**
  Race to the top of the mountain! See the inside of an alien fortress!

C   C   C   C   C   G

Do you wanna know, do you really wanna know how to get to Goon Holler?

G   G   G   G   G   G   C

It's kind of far so don't get mad or hot under your collar.

Go right at the dell, left at the well, wade through muddy creek.

Then you know which way to go, right up Turkey Peak!

(C) (F) (F) (C) (C) (G)
Goon Holler is far away, but if you go this way

(G) (C) (C) (C) (F) (C) (G)
you'll get there. (Come on! I promise that you'll get there!)

(C) (C) (C) (C) (C) (C) (G)

1 fersee 2 fersee 3 fersee 4, climb up the tree that's taller.

(G) (G) (G) (G) (G) (G) (G) (G) (G) (C)

Jump right through a waterfall, and that's how you get to Goon Holler!

Want to meet
the GOON-FOLK?
Turn the page . . .

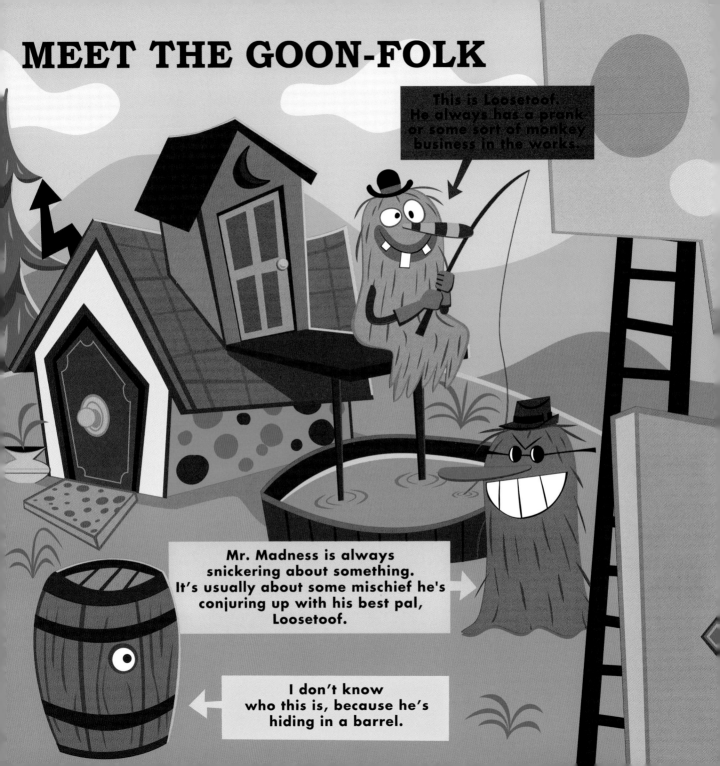

Slapsie Yeller is a little slaphappy because he's the current Goon Holler Slap-Off champion.

Little Finny and Hudley always beat me to the ice cream truck.

If you try to tell Naylor that there's a banana in his ear, he can't hear you because there's a banana in his ear.

Dizzy Bizzy is the best cook I've ever known. EVER!

This is Eefin. He's also known as "Paw," because he's sort of the father of the goons here. He's a hot-roddin' hillbilly!

Hey Bizzy! I smell something yummy in the kitchen. Can we come inside and see what's cookin'?

KITCHEN FIXINS

NAYLOR'S FAVORITE BANANA PUDDING

1 cup sour cream
1 (8 oz) container frozen whipped topping, thawed
1 (5 oz) package instant vanilla pudding mix
2 cups whole milk
1 (16 oz) package vanilla wafer cookies
4 bananas, peeled and sliced

In a large bowl, combine sour cream, whipped topping, pudding mix, and milk. Stir well. In the bottom of a trifle bowl or other glass serving dish, spread a layer of cookies, then a layer of pudding mixture, then a layer of bananas. Repeat until all ingredients are used. Refrigerate until serving. Do not add sardines. That would be disgusting.

ALIEN TENTACLE CRAWLERS

1/2 box dry spaghetti
1/2 package hot dogs

1. Slice hot dogs.
2. Break noodles into multiple pieces.
3. Poke several noodles through each individual hot dog slice.
4. Throw into a big pot of water.
5. Set to boil.
6. Drain and serve when noodles are floppy and cooked through.

LYMAN CUCUMBER PUNCH

1 2-liter bottle of lemon-lime soda
1 punch bowl of crushed ice
1/2 small cucumber

Fill punch bowl with frozen limeade and crushed ice, and add lemon-lime soda to fill bowl. Garnish with cucumber slices. Do a "cahool" dance while stirring. Serve.

MARSHMALLOW GOON PIE

1 package (2-layer size) Devil's Food cake mix
3 squares baker's semi-sweet chocolate, melted
1 (3.9 oz) package chocolate instant pudding
1 (8 oz) package cream cheese, softened
1 cup marshmallow creme
1 (8 oz) tub whipped topping, thawed

1. Heat oven to 350 degrees.
2. Prepare cake mix as directed on package, except use 3/4 cup oil. Add dry pudding mix and melted chocolate, then stir.
3. Drop batter, 2 inches apart, into 20 mounds on baking sheets sprayed with cooking spray, using 1 Tbsp. batter for each.
4. Bake 8 to 10 min. or until toothpick inserted in centers comes out clean. Cool 5 min. on baking sheets; remove to wire racks. Cool completely.
5. Mix cream cheese and marshmallow creme in large bowl until well blended. Gently stir in whipped topping. Spread onto 10 cakes; cover with remaining cakes.

CHURRO POPCORN

4 quarts popped popcorn
1 cup butter
2/3 cup sugar
1 tablespoon cinnamon

Place popcorn in a large bowl. In a microwave-safe bowl, combine the butter, sugar, and cinnamon. Microwave on high for 1 minute; stir. Nuke for 1 minute longer or until the butter is melted. Pour over popcorn and toss to coat. Transfer to 2 greased 15 x 10 x 1" baking pans. Bake, uncovered, at 300 degrees for 10 minutes.

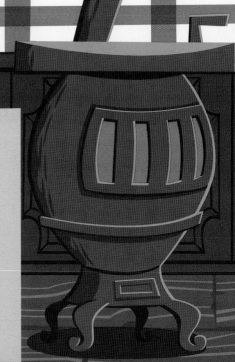

AND THEN THERE'S WHAT RAY CALLED THE **GOONS!**

DID THEY SPRING FROM A HOLE IN THE GROUND?

DID THEY MOVE HERE FROM NEW JERSEY?

OR DID RAY MUTATE A WEIRD FAMILY OF GROUNDHOGS BY MISTAKE?

ZINGO!

THEY FLOURISHED AND MULTIPLIED ALL THROUGH THE HOLLER

AS THOUGH THE MAGIC TOWER WAS THE CENTER OF THEIR NEW VILLAGE

RAY ENJOYED PLAYING WITH HIS NEW NEIGHBORS

BUT GOON DANDER MADE UNCLE WIZNAT SNEEZE

ACHOO!

EVENTUALLY RAY BEGAN TO NOTICE

GOONS ARE CRAZY!

THEY PAINT ON TREES

THEY EAT TIRES

AND THERE'S A MILLION OF THEM IN THE HOLLER!

IN A CONGA LINE!

RAY WONDERED IF HIS CARELESSNESS MIGHT HAVE LED TO THIS CALAMITY KNOWN AS GOON HOLLER, SO HE QUIT MAGIC AND PICKED UP THE GUITAR.

THE END

HOW TO PLAY
SHOOT 'R LOSER

Here's a fun game for two people to play that's similar to "rock, paper, scissors." It's even more fun to play in a big circle of paired-off opponents.

HOW TO PLAY: Face your opponent, clap your hands, ONE ... TWO ... and then on THREE, you make one of the moves below:

SHOOT'R

Point both fingers at your opponent as though you are pretending to shoot. If your opponent is playing the "hands up" move, you win. If your opponent is playing the "deflector" move, you lose.

DEFLECTOR

Hold up your fists with your thumbs extended. If your opponent plays the "Shoot'R" move, point your thumbs forward, bouncing the imaginary bullets back to your opponent. You win!

HANDS UP

Put both hands up into the air as though you are surrendering. If your opponent is playing the Shoot'R move, you just lost. Make a dramatic face. It's more fun that way.

BLOCK

Cross both of your arms over your chest. Pretend you are invincible, because with this move you are safe.

This game has four rounds, and you have to play each move one time. Even though the "hands up" move only makes you vulnerable, use it as a way to taunt your opponent. Then make a silly face.

Keep playing until someone wins. Then play some more!

Shoot'R vs. Block is a draw.

When you put your hands up, just hope your opponent doesn't have his weapons drawn!

Shoot'R vs. Deflector zings your imaginary bullets right back to you.

Here is a simple song to play using the C chord. When you see a mark that looks like ⒸC above the word, that means to strum the uke.

3 SILLY GOONS

To the tune of "Three Blind Mice"

Three silly goons. Three silly goons. Went to the moon.
Went to the moon. They went to go do a jumping jack
but bounced, and flew completely off track.
I wonder if they will ever come back, those three silly goons.

ARE YOU SLEEPING?

To the tune of "Frère Jacques"

FANTASTIC! Now let's try a song with the G chord in it, too!

Ⓒ C · Ⓖ G

Visit Goon Holler online to hear the songs in action!

Are you sleeping? Are you sleeping? Toobaloth? Toobaloth?
You will miss the ice cream. You will miss the ice cream.
You lazy sloth. You lazy sloth.

POOKA SHELLS

The Dolphin
The dolphin is a mermaid's best friend. She is friendly and smart. She smiles even when she is down. She looks so beautiful when she does flips in the air.

The Seahorse
Did you know that a Daddy seahorse carries his babies in a pouch? Go Dad!

The Starfish
Scientists now call it a "Sea Star" because it's technically not a fish. I say, StarFISH!

Sea Dragon
The most wonderful sight underwater. Do Sea Dragons breathe fire?

A guide to a mermaid's favorite underwater creatures

Axolotl
The cutest sea creature of all! She looks like a fish with arms and legs, but she's a salamander. The cutest ones are pink. Some even glow in the dark!

Marshmallow Fish
How many can you fit in your mouth?

Lollirus
The Lollirus is sort of like a walrus, but it has a full head of lollipop hair. Yum!

Flowerfish Jellyfish
Imagine a jellyfish with FLOWERS on it! The perfect gift for your mermaid sweetheart.

Yeti Crab
A furry crustacean that lives deep in the Pacific. He enjoys tap dancing and long walks on the beach.

Octopie
Eight times more delicious than a normal pie!

I SCREAM! YOU SCREAM!

What's your favorite ice cream?

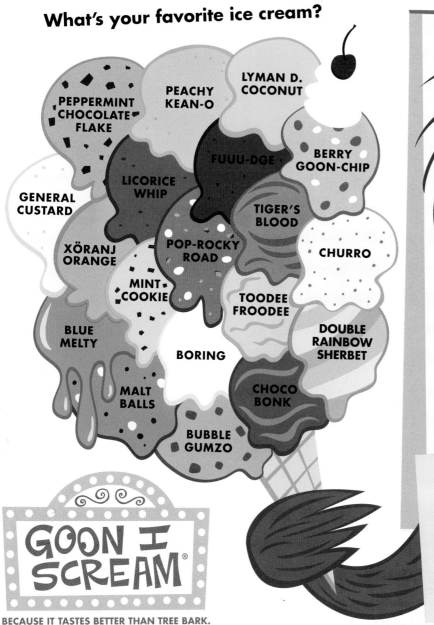

We make so many ice cream flavors that if you ate them all at once, you would totally BARF! But try a different flavor every day, and you'll soon find that they're ALL your favorite!

LYMAN'S GUIDE TO COMEDY

IN TWO EASY STEPS!

STEP 1 • Tell a joke.

If you can't think of a good joke, here are some jokes to start you off.

Why couldn't the tiger tell the truth?
Because he was a lion.

Knock, knock. Who's there?
Cereal. Cereal who?
Cereal pleasure to meet you.

How do you make a witch itch?
Take away her W.

Knock, knock. Who's there?
Dwayne. Dwayne who?
Dwayne da tub, I'm drowning!

Why did the cookie go to the hospital?
It was feeling crummy.

What happens to hairs that break the law?
They get thrown in gel.

What's brown and sticky? A stick!

What did zero say to the number eight? Nice belt!

What kind of gum do bees chew? Bumble gum

What do you call a cow after it has given birth? De-calf-inated

Knock, knock. Who's there? Cereal. Cereal who? Cerealistic impressionists were much better in the Modern Neo-Renaissance period.

What did the finger say to the thumb? I'm in glove with you.

Why is six afraid of seven? Because 7 8 9!

Why was the strawberry mad? He was in a jam!

Knock, knock. Who's there? Interrupting cow. Interrupting cow wh-- MOO!

Who's a chicken's favorite composer? Bach. Bach.

STEP 2 • Hope that your audience laughs.
Good luck with that one!

How do you get an alien baby to sleep? You rocket!

This is JBJB's, my favorite place
to go for a comedy or music show.
It's a great little club
if you can get a table ...

...CAPTURED!?!

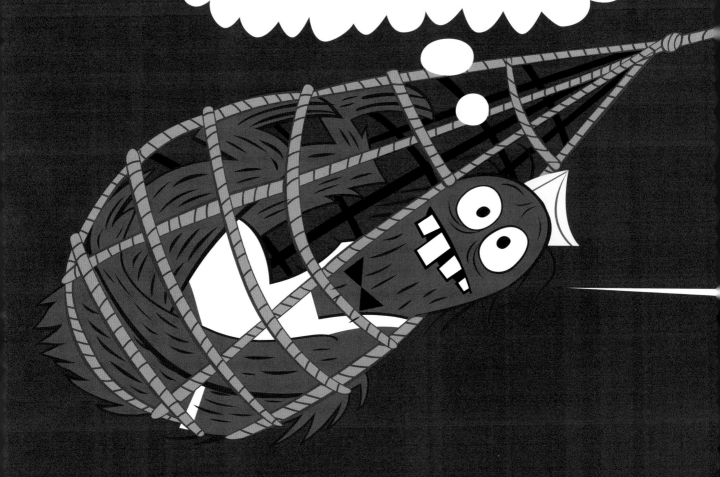

XÖRANJ
(rhymes with orange)
Pilot of the mini-saucer.
He is hoping to repair
the mother ship that
crashed at the top of
Turkey Peak.

GOONBOT RD-RR
Once a normal goon
who loved science
fiction, he's now living
his dream as a cyborg
and servant to his extra-
terrestrial masters.

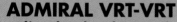

ADMIRAL VRT-VRT
Alien leader, lover of
hard rock, and bitterly
jealous of earthlings.
He hides inside his
booby-trapped mountain
stronghold because he's
afraid of the wild
turkeys outside.

The last time I was here,
Admiral Vrt-Vrt was
really cranky ...

♪ FAREWELL SONG ♪

(C) (C) (C) (F) (F) (F) (F) (C7)
So we say farewell from that lonesome track,

(C7) (C7) (C7) (F) (F) (F) (C7)
Away from Goon Holler, so won't you holler back?

(C7) (F) (F) (C7) (F) (C7)
We'd leave the lights on, but we're not home,

(C) (C) (C) (F)
Here   at   Goon   Holler.